MATH ADVENTURES

HENRY GOES ON A HIKE

A SKIP COUNTING ADVENTURE

by Megan Atwood
illustrated by Amy Zhing

GRASSHOPPER

Tools for Parents & Teachers

Grasshopper Books enhance imagination and introduce the earliest readers to fiction with fun storylines and illustrations. The easy-to-read text supports early reading experiences with repetitive sentence patterns and sight words.

Before Reading

- Look at the cover illustration. What do readers see? What do they think the book will be about?
- Look at the picture glossary together. Sound out the words. Ask readers to identify the first letter of each vocabulary word.

Read the Book

- "Walk" through the book, reading to or along with the reader. Point to the illustrations as you read.

After Reading

- Review the picture glossary again. Ask readers to locate the words in the text.
- Ask the reader: Skip counting helps us count faster. Look around you. What can you skip count?

Grasshopper Books are published by Jump!
5357 Penn Avenue South
Minneapolis, MN 55419
www.jumplibrary.com

Library of Congress Cataloging-in-Publication Data

Names: Atwood, Megan, author. | Zhing, Amy, illustrator.
Title: Henry goes on a hike: a skip counting adventure / by Megan Atwood; illustrated by Amy Zhing.
Description: Minneapolis, MN: Jump!, Inc., [2022]
Series: Math adventures
Audience: Ages 4-7.
Identifiers: LCCN 2021038107 (print)
LCCN 2021038108 (ebook)
ISBN 9781636906324 (hardcover)
ISBN 9781636906331 (paperback)
ISBN 9781636906348 (ebook)
Subjects: LCSH: Readers (Primary)
Counting–Juvenile fiction.
LCGFT: Readers (Publications)
Classification: LCC PE1119.2 .A894 2022 (print)
LCC PE1119.2 (ebook) | DDC 428.6/2–dc23
LC record available at https://lccn.loc.gov/2021038107
LC ebook record available at https://lccn.loc.gov/2021038108

Editor: Eliza Leahy
Direction and Layout: Anna Peterson
Illustrator: Amy Zhing

Printed in the United States of America at Corporate Graphics in North Mankato, Minnesota.

Table of Contents

Let's Skip Count!

Henry and his family go for a hike.

He sees pine cones.

"Let's skip count!" his mom says.

"Skip count?" Henry asks.

“I see four pine cones. One, two, three, four,” his mom says. “Now let’s skip one and three.”

“Two, four!” says Henry.

“That is skip counting by twos!” his mom says.

1 2 3 4

Henry sees swans.

He skip counts by twos.

"Two, four, six, eight!"
he says.

2 4 6 8

Henry sees rocks.

"Can you skip count by threes?" his mom asks.

He makes three groups.

Each has three rocks.

“Nine rocks!” he says.

Henry sees daisies.

“Can you skip count by fives?” his dad asks.

“Yes!” says Henry.

He counts fifteen.

5
10
15

They stop for a snack.

Henry counts apple slices.

"Five, ten, fifteen, twenty . . ." he says. "That means we each get five!"

"That's right!" his dad says.

5
10
15
20

Let's Review!

Count the pine cones below. How many are there? Practice skip counting them by twos, threes, and fours.

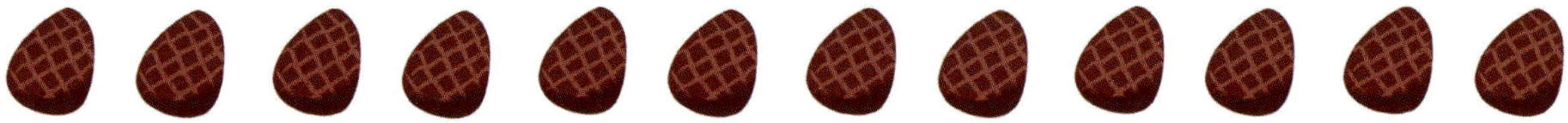

Picture Glossary

groups
Numbers of people or things that go together or have something in common.

hike
A long walk, especially in the country or the mountains.

pine cones
The hard fruit from pine trees.

skip count
To count by numbers other than one.